# PEDRO

## FIRST-CLASS FRIEND

by Fran Manushkin

illustrated by Tammie Lyon

CAPSTONE PRESS
a capstone imprint

Pedro is published by Picture Window Books,
a Capstone Imprint
1710 Roe Crest Drive
North Mankato, Minnesota 56003
www.mycapstone.com

Text © 2018 Fran Manushkin
Illustrations © 2018 Picture Window Books

Cataloging-in-Publication Data is available on the Library of Congress website.

ISBN: 978-1-5158-2840-2

Summary: Pedro is a fun and kind friend. Read about his adventures in this
four-story collection.

Designers: Kayla Rossow and Charmaine Whitman

Design Elements: Shutterstock

Printed and bound in Canada.
PA020

# Table of Contents

# PEDRO'S
# MONSTER

Pedro was dreaming.

He dreamed that a creepy

green dragon was chasing him.

The dragon was blowing flames!

Pedro told his dad about his dream.

His dad said, "Don't worry about it. Dream dragons can't hurt you."

Pedro tried to forget his dream.

He raced his trucks all over the yard.

He and his brother Paco did
speedy donuts, going around and
around. They got nice and dizzy.

Pedro told Paco, "Now I'll jump over the highest hill."

Oops! Pedro went flying and landed in the mud.

"Cool!" he yelled.

The next night, Pedro had
another bad dream. He dreamed that
a long slimy worm was creeping up
his leg!

Pedro's dad told him, "Dream worms cannot hurt you. And I have a nice surprise. I'm taking you and your friends to a monster truck rally."

"Yay!" yelled Pedro. "Cool!"

Pedro and Katie and JoJo painted posters for the rally.

BASH AND SMASH!

MASH AND SMASH!

CRUSH! CRUSH! CRUSH!

They were ready to cheer on the truck drivers.

The next day was the rally.
The first truck did a somersault
and landed in the mud.

*THUD! SPLASH!*

"Awesome!" Pedro yelled. "I did
that too."

A gigantic school bus crushed three cars!

"I'd like to drive that," shouted Katie.

JoJo smiled. "You *would!*"

The trucks were fierce, roaring and doing wheelies around each other.

"Super awesome!" yelled Pedro.

The next day at school, Pedro wrote a story about monster trucks. He could not stop thinking about them.

But Pedro kept having bad
dreams. Each night before bedtime,
Pedro ate cookies, hoping to have
sweet dreams.

He didn't.

Each day after school, Pedro raced his trucks. He went faster and roared louder.

"Go, BIG THUNDER!" Katie cheered.

"That's you!" shouted JoJo. "BIG THUNDER!"

"Right!" yelled Pedro. "I am noisy, and I am fast! Nothing can stop me."

Pedro kept smiling. He smiled all through dinner.

That night at bedtime, Pedro told himself, "I am strong! I am powerful! I am BIG THUNDER!"

Pedro said it again and again until he fell asleep.

Then it happened!

Pedro had a horrible dream. That creepy green dragon began chasing him! The dragon roared and blew his scary flames!

But Pedro didn't run away. He roared back—loud as thunder. Pedro chased that dragon around in circles and into the mud!

The dragon's fire went out! He cried and cried, saying, "You are so fierce!"

Then he ran away.

Katie and JoJo cheered, "Way to go, BIG THUNDER!"

Pedro woke up smiling. He told his mom and dad about his dream.

"You were great, Pedro!" said his mom.

"Way to go!" said his dad.

Pedro couldn't stop smiling.

"You were right," he told his dad. "Dream monsters cannot hurt me."

Then Pedro gobbled up his breakfast—Chocolate Crunch!

# PEDRO'S BIG
# BREAK

Pedro loved going fast. Winning bike races was fun.

He told Katie, "Today I can win my third race in a row. I just need a big break."

*Zoom!* The race began.

Pedro rode fast—very fast!

Oops! His bike hit a rock, and
Pedro went flying. He fell hard on
his arm!

The doctor told him, "Your arm is broken, but this cast will help it heal. You'll be fine in four weeks."

Pedro groaned. "This *isn't* the big break I wanted."

Pedro told Katie, "Now I can't go camping. I'll miss sleeping in a tent and eating s'mores and seeing shooting stars."

"I'll draw stars on your cast,"
said Katie. "Then you can see them
all the time."

But Pedro still felt sad. He
wasn't fast anymore. He had to do
everything slowly.

Taking a bath was tricky. Getting dressed was tricky too.

In school, Pedro had to write with his wrong hand.

Miss Winkle tried to cheer him up. She said, "Your bone will heal in just a few weeks."

Pedro groaned. "I want it to happen faster."

JoJo told Pedro, "Your arm is
broken, but your brain still works.
I bet you will think of ways to be
happy."

But Pedro kept thinking about the camping trip he was missing.

No shooting stars!

No scary stories!

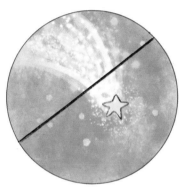

No s'mores!

A week later, Pedro's brother Paco woke up in the middle of the night. He told Pedro, "I had a scary dream!"

Paco cried and cried.

Pedro wanted to cheer Paco up.
Wrestling always made him happy,
but Pedro couldn't wrestle.

"What can I do with one hand?"
he wondered.

"Aha!" Pedro smiled. "I know!"

Pedro made funny shadow puppets. One hand could do a lot!

Paco laughed and laughed and forgot his dream. Soon he hugged his pillow and fell asleep smiling.

Before he fell back to sleep, Pedro had another fun idea. "We can camp in the yard!"

But when Pedro woke up, it was raining. The ground was all wet.

"I know," said Pedro. "Let's camp inside. My sheet can be our tent."

"Cool idea," said his dad.

His mom made a campfire out of colored paper.

"A camp needs ants," said Katie. She made ants on  a log by filling celery with peanut butter and raisins.

"Yum," said Pedro. "These ants are tasty."

JoJo told scary stories, and they spooked each other with flashlights. Then they ate lots of s'mores.

Pedro said, "All we are missing are shooting stars."

"No way," said his dad. "I'll get the telescope. We can see shooting stars right here."

Pedro's dad placed his telescope near the window.

"I see them!" Pedro yelled. "I see shooting stars. Boy, are they fast!"

Boy, was Pedro happy!

"Next week," said his dad, "your cast is coming off."

"Yay!" everyone cheered.

Pedro cheered the loudest.

A few weeks later, Pedro was racing again—fast, fast, fast!

"From now on," he said, "I don't want to get any more big breaks."

And so far, he hasn't!

# ON TOP OF THE WORLD

"Yay!" yelled Pedro. "We are finally at Family Fun Park. Let's stay all day. It's great at night too."

Pedro, Katie, and JoJo loved riding the Tilt-and-Twirl.

"Spin faster!" yelled Pedro.

"I'm dizzy!" yelled Katie.

"I'm not," said Pedro.

Then they rode the Rapid River
Flume. The ride was fierce and fast.

"That was fun," said Pedro. "But
I want a scary ride."

"Here's a wild ride," said Pedro's dad. "Let's try the Ferris Wheel."

Pedro watched the big wheel spinning, rising high into the sky. "Hmm," he said. "Maybe later."

"I want cotton candy!" yelled
Pedro's brother, Paco.

"I see popcorn!" said Pedro. "Can
we get some?"

Pedro's mom took Paco to get cotton candy. Pedro and his dad walked the other way to get popcorn.

The line for popcorn was very
long. It took a while to get some.

"Now," said Pedro's dad, "let's go
back to your mom and the others."

They found Katie and JoJo eating
ice cream with Katie's mom.

"Have you seen my mom and
Paco?" asked Pedro.

"No," said Katie.

Pedro and his dad searched and searched. Finally, they found Pedro's mom. She was searching too!

"A parade came by," she said, "and Paco got lost in the crowd."

"I'll tell the lost and found," said Katie's mom.

"The rest of us will keep searching," said Pedro's dad. "We have to hurry. It will be dark soon."

"I have an idea!" said Pedro's dad. "Let's take a ride on the Ferris Wheel. From high up, we can see the whole park. It's a fast way to find Paco."

"I can't," said Pedro. "It's too scary!"

Pedro began walking away. But then he came back. "My brother is in trouble!" he said. "I have to be brave."

When the wheel began spinning, Pedro held his dad's hand. Up went the big wheel, higher and higher and *HIGHER*!

At the top, it stopped!

"Yikes!" yelled Pedro's dad. "I'm not wild about this."

He closed his eyes. But Pedro kept his eyes open. There was so much to see!

"Dad," Pedro yelled, "open your eyes! This is *fun,* and I can see Paco!"

"Wow!" Pedro's dad smiled. "This is awesome!"

After a few more spins, Pedro and
his dad were back on the ground.
Pedro led his dad to Paco.

Oh, was there hugging!

"I was in a parade!" bragged Paco. "This park is fun!"

"Sometimes," said his dad.

"Always!" yelled Pedro. "I was brave. *Boy*, was I brave!"

Soon everyone was back together.

"Before we go," said Katie,
"let's all ride the Cannonball Roller
Coaster."

"Yikes!" said Pedro's mom. "That's high—and FAST."

"Don't worry," said Pedro's dad. "If you take Pedro, he will help you be brave."

And he did!

# THE BIG
# STINK

"Today," said Miss Winkle,

"we will study our sense of smell."

"I should get my cat," said JoJo.

"Her breath is smelly."

"No thanks," said Miss Winkle.

"My dad's gym socks are stinky,"
said Katie. "I can bring them."

"No thanks again," said Miss
Winkle.

"Our noses can pick out a trillion smells," said Miss Winkle. "Let's see if you can guess some. Pablo will pass them out."

Pablo was the new boy. He was kind of quiet.

Katie Woo sniffed and said,
"This smells like a
pencil."

"Smart sniffing!"
said Miss Winkle.
"But polar bears have better noses
than humans. They can smell a seal
through three feet of ice."

"My dog can smell a burger in his sleep," bragged Pedro. He smelled his box. "I smell a potato chip," he said.

"Pew!" yelled Barry. "I got onions!"

Then it was time for lunch. Pedro and Pablo ate together.

Pedro traded half of his cheese sandwich for part of Pablo's taco.

After lunch, everyone played soccer. When Pablo got the ball, Roddy yelled, "Beat it, shrimp! You're too small to play with us."

Pedro didn't say anything.

After lunch, Miss Winkle told
the class, "While I was eating, I was
thinking of funny ways we talk about
smells. When we don't trust someone,
we say, 'I smell a rat.'"

"Hey," said Pedro, sniffing, "I smell something stinky right now."

"Me too," said JoJo.

"Me three," yelled Roddy.

"Maybe," said Miss Winkle. "I'm not sure."

Everyone began sniffing and searching.

"It's not coming from Binky," said Barry. "His cage is clean."

"So is our turtle's," said Katie.

"It's Pablo!" Roddy pointed.
"Our classroom never smelled until
he came."

Everyone stared at Pablo. He
looked like he might cry. Nobody
said anything.

At first, Pedro was quiet too.

But then he stood up. He said,
"Pablo does not stink. But I know
what does: It's when we don't stick up
for someone who is being picked on."

Roddy turned red. He said,
"I was only joking."

"No you weren't," said Katie.
"And that hurt."

"I'm sorry," Roddy told Pablo.
They shook hands on it.

Suddenly Katie yelled, "I know
what that smell is: It's a rotten egg."

"Ew!" said JoJo.

"Pew!" yelled everyone else.

"We have to find it!" said Pedro.
He and Pablo searched together.

Pablo pointed. "That's where it's
coming from: Miss Winkle's closet!"

Miss Winkle ran over and opened
the door. She grabbed her purse and
found something in the bottom.

"Oh my!" she said. "Here's the
rotten egg!"

"I brought it for lunch yesterday but I ate a hot lunch instead. I have a cold today, so I couldn't smell it."

Miss Winkle said, "Roddy and
Pablo, please toss out this rotten egg."

"Easy peasy," said Roddy.

"Easy peasy." Pablo smiled.

After school, they played soccer.
Roddy told Pablo, "You are small,
but quick!"

Pablo told Roddy, "You are pretty
good too."

"Sometimes," said Roddy.

When Pedro got home, he told his dad, "Ask me how school was today."

"How was it?" asked his dad.

"It was smelly!" Pedro smiled, and he told him all about it.

# JOKE AROUND

★ What's big and scary
and has three wheels?
a monster riding
on a tricycle

★ Why do dragons sleep during
the day?
So they can fight knights.

★ What kind of horses do
monsters ride?
night mares

★ What do you say
when you meet a
two-headed monster?
"Bye-bye."

★ Why did the book go to
the doctor?
It broke its spine.

★ How did the frog feel when
it had a broken leg?
unhoppy

★ What is the most musical bone?
the trom-bone

★ What do you do for a bird
with a broken wing?
Give it special
tweet-ment.

# JOKE AROUND

★ Why did the chicken cross the amusement park? to get to the other ride

★ Why didn't the skeleton ride the roller coaster? He didn't have the guts.

★ Do fish like to visit amusement parks? No, they are always in school!

★ What is a frog's favorite treat at the amusement park? hopsicles

★ Have you heard the joke about the skunk? It really stinks.

★ What smells the best at dinner? your nose

★ Why can't a nose be 12 inches long? Because then it would be a foot.

★ Knock, knock
Who's there?
Nose
Nose who?
I nose plenty more knock-knock jokes, don't worry!

## About the Author

Fran Manushkin is the author of many popular picture books, including *Happy in Our Skin; Baby, Come Out!; Latkes and Applesauce: A Hanukkah Story; The Tushy Book; Big Girl Panties; Big Boy Underpants;* and *Bamboo for Me, Bamboo for You!* There is a real Katie Woo—she's Fran's great-niece—but she never gets in half the trouble of the Katie Woo in the books. Fran writes on her beloved Mac computer in New York City, without the help of her two naughty cats, Chaim and Goldy.

## About the Illustrator

Tammie Lyon began her love for drawing at a young age while sitting at the kitchen table with her dad. She continued her love of art and eventually attended the Columbus College of Art and Design, where she earned a bachelor's degree in fine art. After a brief career as a professional ballet dancer, she decided to devote herself full time to illustration. Today she lives with her husband, Lee, in Cincinnati, Ohio. Her dogs, Gus and Dudley, keep her company as she works in her studio.